Green Light Readers
For the new reader who's ready to GO!

Amazing adventures await every young child who is eager to read.

Green Light Readers encourage children to explore, to imagine, and to grow through books. Created for beginning readers at two levels of skill, these lively illustrated stories have been carefully developed to reinforce reading basics taught at school and to make reading a fun and rewarding experience for children and grown-ups to share outside the classroom.

The grades and ages within each skill level are general guidelines only, and books included in both levels may feature any or all of the bulleted characteristics. When choosing a book for a new reader, remember that every child progresses at his or her own pace—be patient and supportive as the magic of reading takes hold.

❶ Buckle up!
Kindergarten–Grade 1: Developing reading skills, ages 5–7
- Short, simple stories • Fully illustrated • Familiar objects and situations
- Playful rhythms • Spoken language patterns of children
- Rhymes and repeated phrases • Strong link between text and art

2 Start the engine!
Grades 1–2: Reading with help, ages 6–8
- Longer stories, including nonfiction • Short chapters
- Generously illustrated • Less-familiar situations
- More fully developed characters • Creative language, including dialogue
- More subtle link between text and art

Green Light Readers incorporate characteristics detailed in the Reading Recovery model used by educators to assess the readability of texts through the end of first grade. Guidelines for reading levels for these readers have been developed with assistance from Mary Lou Meerson. An educational consultant, Ms. Meerson has been a classroom teacher, a language arts coordinator, an elementary school principal, and a university professor.

Published in collaboration with Harcourt School Publishers

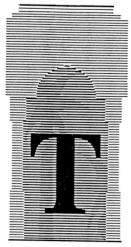

Sam and Jack

Three Stories

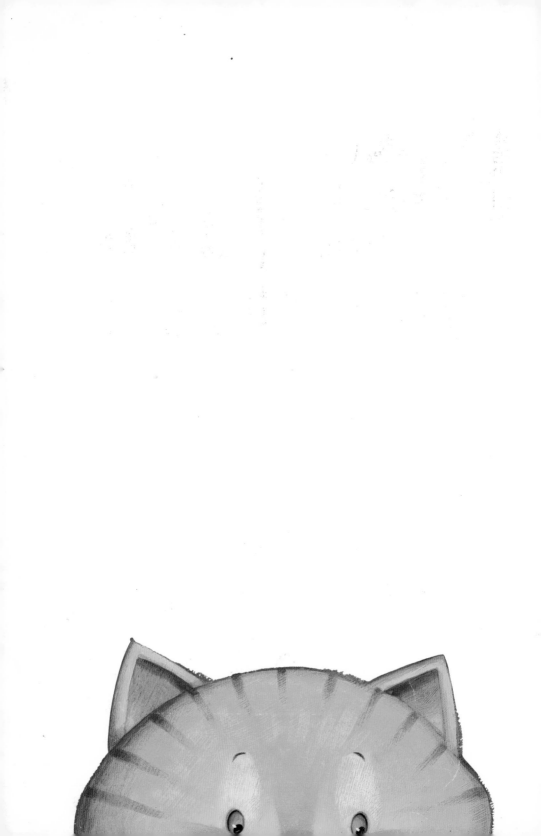

Sam and Jack
Three Stories

Alex Moran

Illustrated by Tim Bowers

Green Light Readers
Harcourt, Inc.
San Diego New York London

www.harcourt.com

First Green Light Readers edition 2001
Green Light Readers is a trademark of Harcourt, Inc., registered
in the United States of America and/or other jurisdictions.

Library of Congress Cataloging-in-Publication Data
Moran, Alex.
Sam and Jack/Alex Moran; illustrated by Tim Bowers.
p. cm.
"Green Light Readers."
Summary: Sam the mouse and Jack the cat overcome
their differences and become friends.
[1. Cats—Fiction. 2. Mice—Fiction. 3. Friendship—Fiction.]
I. Bowers, Tim, ill. II. Title.
PZ7.M788193Sam 2001
[E]—dc21   2001000413
ISBN 0-15-216240-2
ISBN 0-15-216234-8 (pb)

A C E G H F D B
A C E G H F D B (pb)

A Surprise

I see a mat.

I see a hat on a mat.

I see a tail on a mat.

I see a cat on a mat.

It is Jack the cat!

Jack

Are you a cat?

I am a cat.

Are you a friend?

I am a friend.

I am your funny friend, Jack.

Sam

I am Sam.

I am little.

I am big.

I am sad.

I am happy.

Meet the Illustrator

Tim Bowers loves to draw pictures of animals. Dogs were his favorite animal to paint when he was a young boy. He painted many pictures of his own dog, which still hang in his parents' house today! Now he enjoys drawing all sorts of different animals.